Starting off with

Counting

Written by Peter Patilla

Illustrations by Liz Pichon

BARRON'S

First edition for the United States and its dependencies published 2001
by Barron's Educational Series, Inc.

Originally published 2000 by Oxford University Press.

Text © Peter Patilla 2000
Illustrations © Liz Pichon 2000

The moral rights of the author and illustrator have been asserted.

All inquiries should be addressed to:
Barron's Educational Series, Inc.
250 Wireless Boulevard
Hauppauge, New York 11788
http://www.barronseduc.com

International Standard Book No. 0-7641-1657-6

Library of Congress Catalog Card No. 00-102970

PRINTED IN HONG KONG
9 8 7 6 5 4 3 2 1

My name is

....

Notes for parents and teachers

This book develops early concepts of *counting* for adults and children to enjoy and share together. It has been carefully written to introduce the key words and ideas related to *counting* that children will meet in their first couple of years in school.

Throughout the book, you will see **Word Banks** that contain the new math terms introduced for each concept. All the words from the word banks are gathered together at the back of the book. You can use the word banks with your child in several ways:

- See which of the words are recognized through games such as *I spy. I spy the word "twenty"—can you find it? I spy a word beginning with "z"—where is it?*
- Choose a word and ask your child to find it in the book.
- Let your child choose a word from the word bank at the back of the book, and say something about it.

Look for other opportunities in everyday life to use the ideas and vocabulary introduced in this book. Count items when shopping, talk about which order the numbers go in, and pick out words and numbers in your own writing and conversation. Make sure that children realize that counting is easy, and most importantly, fun.

Counting up

We use these numbers when we count forward.

0 zero   1 one   2 two   3 three

4 four   5 five   6 six   7 seven

8 eight   9 nine   10 ten

| 0 | 1 | 2 | 3 | 4 | 5 | 6 | 7 | 8 | 9 | 10 |

Add one more

Numbers get larger when we count forward.

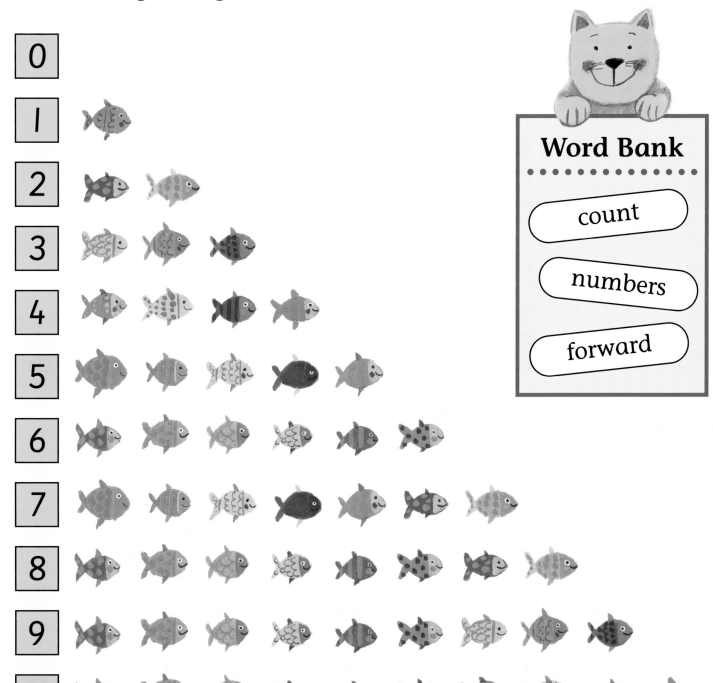

0
1
2
3
4
5
6
7
8
9
10

Word Bank

count

numbers

forward

0
1
2
3
4
5

Counting backward

We use these numbers when we count backward.

10 ten

9 nine

8 eight

7 seven

6 six

5 five

4 four

3 three

2 two

1 one

0 zero

| 10 | 9 | 8 | 7 | 6 | 5 | 4 | 3 | 2 | 1 | 0 |

Count one back

Numbers get smaller when we count back.

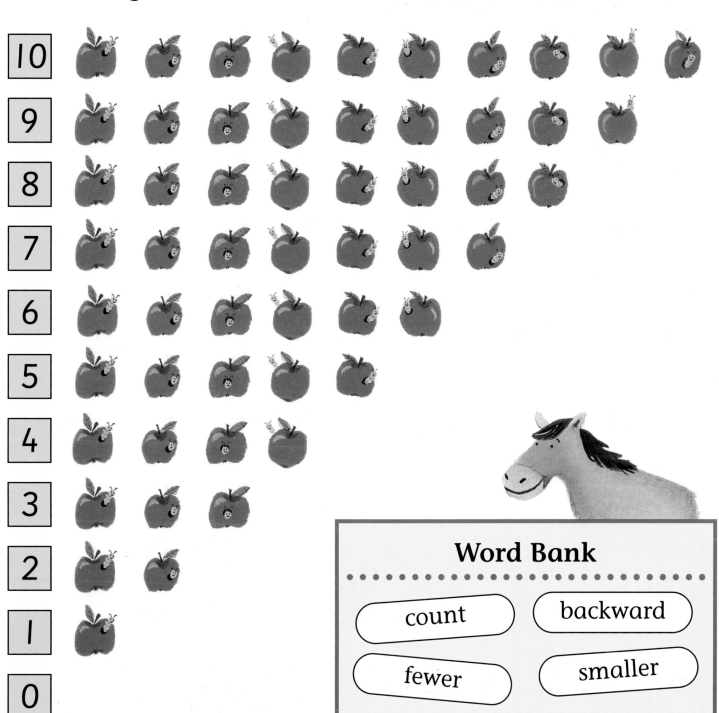

Word Bank

count   backward

fewer   smaller

Counting how many

Counting tells us how many things there are.

| 0 | 1 | 2 | 3 | 4 | 5 | 6 | 7 | 8 | 9 | 10 |

... and counting in twos

Counting in twos is quicker than counting in ones.
How many shoes are in each rack?

Word Bank

count

twos

altogether

total

how many?

0 1 2 3 4 5

Counting and comparing

Rearranging things does not make the number different.

Counting is easier when things are tidy.

When things are spread out they can look like more.

Counting in twos is quicker than counting in ones.

Count each set. Check that they are the same.

... and checking

Count and check whether these sets are the same.

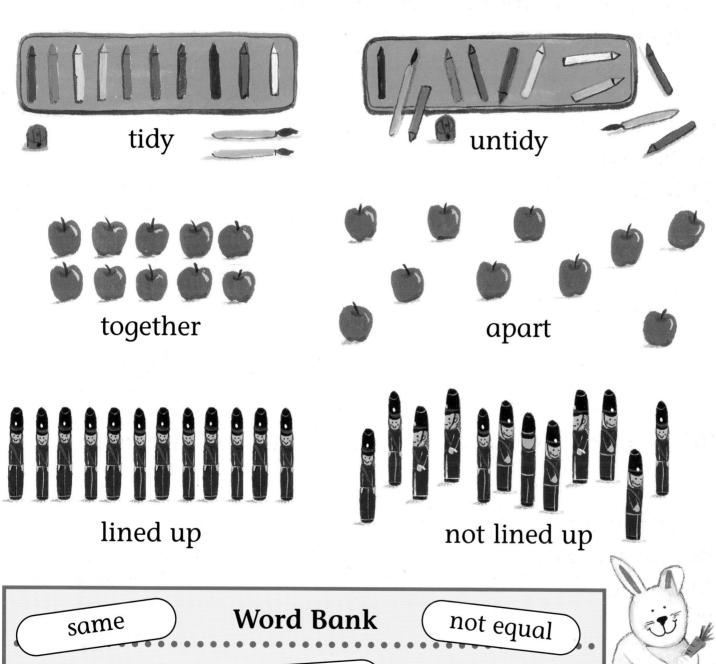

tidy

untidy

together

apart

lined up

not lined up

Word Bank

same   not equal

equal   match   how many?

More or fewer

We can count to see whether there are more or fewer things.

There are more red apples than green.

There are fewer ducks than swans.

There are more green apples than red.

There are fewer butterflies than bees.

There are more short flowers than tall flowers.

There are fewer swans than ducks.

... and the same

Amy Craig Sam Carrie Ross

Who has fewer pencils?

Who has more bricks?
Who has the same?

Are there enough coats for the children?
Will there be too many hats?
Are there more pairs of boots than hats?

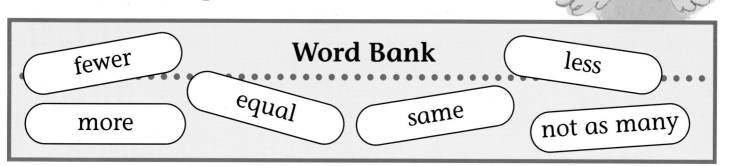

Word Bank

fewer

less

more

equal

same

not as many

Number signs

We use the signs **<**, **>**, and **=** to compare numbers.

This sign **>** means more than.

6 > 4
six is more than four

This sign **<** means less than.

8 < 10
eight is less than ten

This sign **=** means the same as or equals.

 **+**  **=**

3 + 2 = 5
three plus two equals five

... and comparing numbers

A set can be more, less, or equal to another.

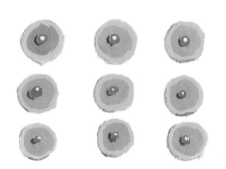

Is this set more or less than the other?

Is this set less or more than the other?

Word Bank

more

fewer

less

greater

equal

same

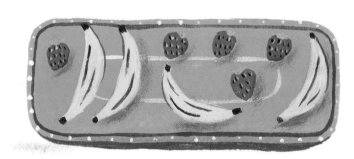

Are the sets the same?

Ordering things

We use words such as first, second, and third to order things.

10th
9th
8th
7th
6th
5th
4th
3rd
2nd
1st

fifth
5th

fourth
4th

third
3rd

second
2nd

first
1st

last

middle

first

... and lines

When we stand in a line there is an order.

Who is first? Who is last?

Who is 1st? Who is 3rd? Who is 6th?

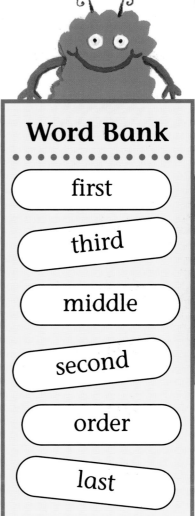

Who is at the start? Who is at the end?
Who is in the middle?

Numerals

Numerals can be numbers,
words, or signs.

Numerals are used to show how many are in a set.
Here are some numerals.

numbers	words	tallies	digital numbers
0	zero		0
1	one	I	1
2	two	II	2
3	three	III	3
4	four	IIII	4
5	five	ⅢⅡ	5
6	six	ⅢⅡ I	6
7	seven	ⅢⅡ II	7
8	eight	ⅢⅡ III	8
9	nine	ⅢⅡ IIII	9
10	ten	ⅢⅡ ⅢⅡ	10

... and numbers

We see numerals in all sorts of places.
Which of these numerals do you recognize?

How old is each child?

Which is the highest number?

Word Bank

numeral

number

tally

sign

word

symbol

Who has scored the most?

Tens

We count large numbers in tens.

0		zero
10		ten
20		twenty
30		thirty
40		forty
50		fifty
60		sixty
70		seventy
80		eighty
90		ninety
100		hundred

Can you see the pattern of fives?

... and patterns

Counting large numbers is easier when they are in a pattern. You do not always have to count in ones. Guess, then count how many are in each of these patterns.

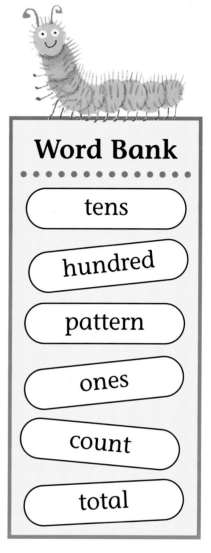

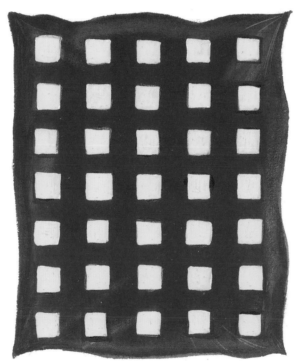

Word Bank

- tens
- hundred
- pattern
- ones
- count
- total

Number sequences

Numbers are often written in order on tracks and grids.

Number tracks can go on and on and on ....

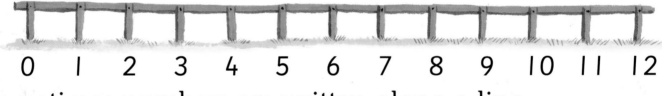

0   1   2   3   4   5   6   7   8   9   10   11   12

Sometimes numbers are written along a line.

Number grids are used when there are lots of numbers.

1	2	3	4	5	6	7	8	9	10
11	12	13	14	15	16	17	18	19	20
21	22	23	24	25	26	27	28	29	30
31	32	33	34	35	36	37	38	39	40
41	42	43	44	45	46	47	48	49	50
51	52	53	54	55	56	57	58	59	60
61	62	63	64	65	66	67	68	69	70

... and jumping

Number tracks help us count ahead and back.

This shows counting ahead 4.

This shows counting back 4.

Word Bank

- tens
- hundred
- pattern
- ones
- count ahead
- count back

It is easy to spot the missing numbers in a grid.

Which numbers are missing?

1	2	3	4	5	6	7	8	9	10
11	12		14	15	16	17	18	19	
21	22	23	24	25	26		28	29	30
31	32	33	34	35	36	37	38		40
41	42	43		45	46	47	48	49	50
	52	53	54	55	56		58	59	60
61		63	64	65	66	67	68	69	

23

Ordering numbers

Numbers are often written in an order.

Sometimes numbers go around and then start all over again.

Numbers can be arranged so that we know where they are.

Sometimes numbers go on for quite a long way.

Numbers sometimes go up in twos.

... and positions

You will see numbers written in an order in all sorts of places.

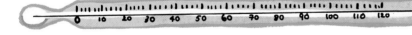

Word Bank

- order
- position
- next to
- before
- after
- between

off they went..

What will the next two pages be?

Counting long ago

People have found different ways of counting.

Many years ago people used different things to help them count.
We still use some of these ways today.

fingers

fingers and toes

stones and seeds

tally marks

tally sticks

simple abacus

... and writing

People have written numbers in all sorts of different ways.

marks in clay

picture signs

Roman numerals

zero was first used in India

numbers on slate and paper

calculators and computers

Word Bank

Do you remember these words?
Can you find them in the book?

count

1 2 3

forward

numbers

3 2 1

backward

greater

smaller

fewer

altogether

how many?

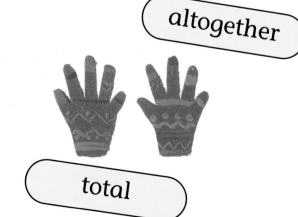

total

Word Bank

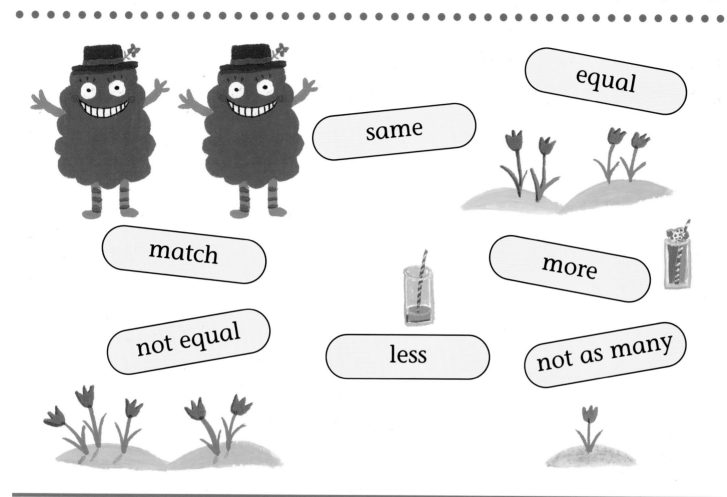

equal

same

match

more

not equal

less

not as many

tens

ones

twos

hundred

Word Bank

first

second

third

order

1

2

3

numeral

symbol

tally

number

sign

− +

pattern

word

30

Word Bank

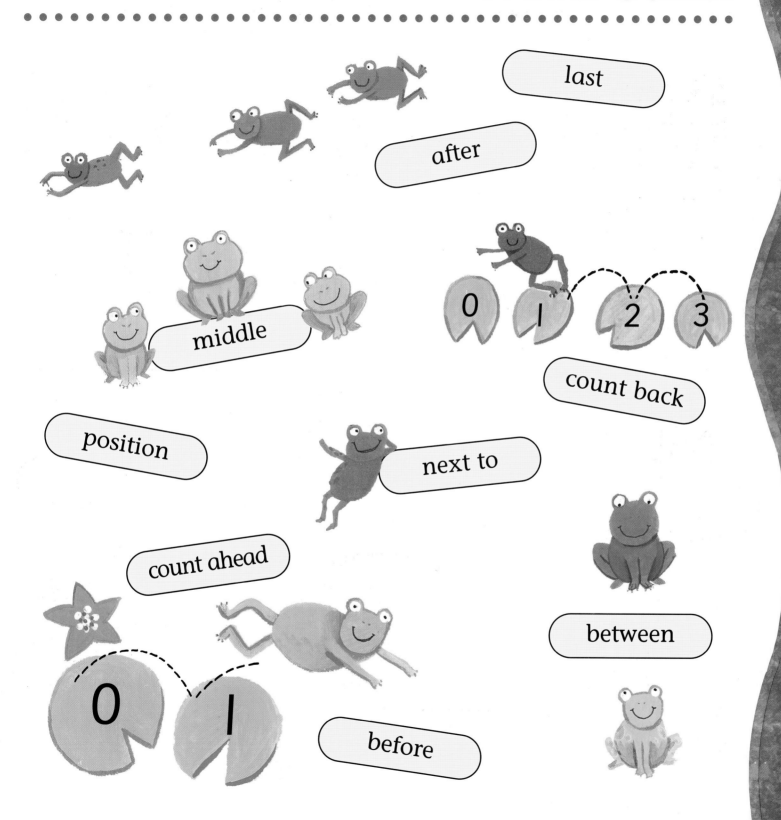

last

after

middle

position

count back

next to

count ahead

between

before

Counting Quiz

Which is less, 11 or 13?

How many toes are on 4 feet?

Which number comes after 13? Which numbers come between 10 and 13?

Who is last?

Which number comes before 20?

Which number comes next?

10 20 30 40

Which is more, 15 or 17?